Many thanks go to the late Phil 'Doc' Dockerty.
He turned his talents to creating a song from the
Music Magic poem. May he rest in peace knowing how
honoured I feel.
To Claire Tomlinson, the staff, the musicians
and local patrons of the
Ye Olde John O Gaunt pub in Lancaster UK
for their unwavering support.
To Nick Hogton, my beautiful man, my saviour,
my rock, my husband.
And to my son Stuart Ridley and his family for
putting up with this crazy old woman.
Thank you, thank you and thrice thank you all.

Words of Whimsy

Welcome to my first book.

This is a collection of poetry
that I have written over the last few years.
I hope you find my work thought provoking
and ultimately uplifting

Chapter One.............Nature's Bounty
Chapter Two............A Journey Through Grief
Chapter Three..........The Love Of Music
Chapter Four...........The Life Of A Carer
Chapter Five............Pure Whimsy

Chapter One

Nature's bounty

Chapter 1 Contents

1....I Wish I Had A Garden
2....The Storm
3....Autumn
4....I Asked The North Wind
5... English Sun
6....Love Is In The Detail
7....A Million Kisses
8....Sunshine
9....Sprinkles
10...Blue Butterfly

1 I Wish I Had a Garden

I wish I had a garden
A peaceful place to be
To listen to some birdsong
underneath an apple tree
I wish I had a bench.
Upon which I'd sit and dwell
I'd think on how this life has changed
Now the world has gone to hell
I wish I had my family
My Uncle and my Gran
But they got taken off this day
In a medical type van
I wish I had a party
All the rabble at the bar
But drinking ale and singing song's
Is a social step too far
We need to kill this C word
Each warrior on their own
We will fight our mental battles
From the safety of our homes
We ought to use the media
To check on all our friends
To save our fears and sing our songs
Until this nightmare ends

We have to practice abstinence from most
things that we know. We have to stay behind
our gates or the plague will never go
We need to follow simple rules if we are going to win
Be safe, be kind, don't lose your mind
Lets pour another gin

2 The Storm

A storm is brewing, the pressure is high
The dark clouds gather as I look to the sky

The trees start to rustle, the green leaves shimmer
And all the while the light it grows dimmer

The birds fall silent. The sky gives a moan
This is the time to head for your home

But not for the wild ones, not for the witch
They feed of the power it scratches an itch

Then flash goes the lightning and down comes the rain
The thunderclaps roar like the earth is in pain

The wild ones are laughing in manic delight
The rain turns to hail in a show of pure spite

And then it's all over as fast as begun
The ground smells of perfume
on return of the sun

The witch dries her feet and returns to her home
The feeling is sweet
Nature's work has been done

3   Autumn

Autumn is coming with death all around
From our fallen friends to leaves on the ground
The flowers are fading the fruits getting fat
The local cat chasing another damn rat

Yes autumn is coming the sky's growing dark
We wrap up our coats to take kids to the park
We wrap up our homes light the fires get warm
But don't forget folks autumn has other forms

Yes Autumn is coming leaves are gold like on fire
The sunset lights up silhouettes of a spire
The promise of cocoa and hugs by the hearth
With cosy old melodies played after dark

Yes Autumn is coming fear not my good friend
As everything truly must come to an end
An end to the summer, yes end to the sun
But a new time of wonder and life has begun

A new time of harvest, nuts on the tree
Of warm mulled wine, of birds flying free
A time of pubs and friends gathered together
A time to be thankful whatever the weather

4 I asked the North Wind

I asked the North wind 'where do you come from?'
Is it a mountain tops blast, snow melting in sun?
Or a giant on a fjord blowing farts just for fun?
Needless to say no answer did come.

I asked the sea 'where did the land end?'
'Did the rivers cut it up? Did we do something to offend?
Or did the water nymphs feel it didn't quite blend?'
No answer again heaven forfend

I asked the fire ' why do you consume?
Why do you destroy? Why so angry? Why fume? '
So sorry do we spin our web on Satan's loom?
No answers again I guess I'm just a loon

I asked the Earth 'why slip and slide
When you provide so much and give such pride? '
The fae have been seen far and wide
And yet again the answers do hide

I asked my spirit 'why dont I understand?
Why do the answers evade my hand?'
The giants, the nymphs, the fae are real
I hear Satan jeer 'live however you feel'

In conclusion dear reader I have to say
I love a little lunacy at the end of the day
It helps the mind deal with everyday pains
So tomorrow perhaps we can all laugh again.

5   English Sun

Some people love the heat of the sun
Some folks prefer gentle rain
As for myself it's like hell has come
And every hour causes pain

But still we gather in our droves
To beaches, parks and camps
And make the most of this one week
before the return to damp

The English Sun is a fickle beast
Always there but rarely felt
We plan our little picnic feast
Then bang our skin starts to melt

I should be grateful it's just one week
And the rest of the year we will moan
I just wish the heat was a little more meek
And we are able to sleep in our homes

But to conclude this lyrical rant
I wish to share all the love the sun brings
I gift all good vibes to you reader, but recant
English Sun is just not my thing

6 Love is in the Detail

The devil's in the detail.
The same is true of love
Its not the grandest gesture
Its not money from above

Its the little things that matter
A smile, a touch, a kiss
You don't have to be a mad hatter
To create a spot of bliss

Pay attention to their likes and loves
Pay attention to their woes
Just let them know its them you love
And its not just all for show

So friends I wish for you this day
Your souls to be set free,
For a little love along the way
And to be happy just like me

7   A Million Kisses

A million kisses on my face
As the rain comes down I feel out of place
An equal share of tiny pains
That build in strength again and again

I'm waiting on my tardy bus
To get me home without a fuss
I'm waiting on my husbands arms
This rotten weather does me harm

But soon I'll shake the damp and gloom
Get snuggled up in my living room
To think about another day
When maybe sunshine will come my way

But until then I stand and wait
Inside the shelter near a gate
Hurry up bus I'm nearly beat
But the million kisses were kinda sweet

8 Sunshine

Sunshine feeling fine, eat the food, drink the wine
Soon it's gonna be party time
Wake in the morning, smile on my face
Remembering fun, that's not normally the case
Laughing with friends the night before
If laughter is currency I'm normally poor
But today I feel great I've lost all the hate
I've a warm glow within and feel good in my skin
It's strange but it's true wow I don't feel blue
Tonight will be fun good sounds maybe rum
A few friendly faces more drink, better pace it
I'll laugh and just be for all to see
A woman transformed flying high loving life
and not just a sad and lone grieving wife
So bring on the day sun shine on me
and help me to stay a happier me
bring on the night no need to fight
The beast has been slain
No head pain tonight
No tears, no remorse
Just steer a straight course out of grief into fun
New life has begun
And all because of good friends
And the sun

9 Sprinkles

Sprinkles and sparkles and all things I hate
Carol singers howling at my garden gate
Tinsel and glitter, the devil's dandruff
And everyone happy good grief that's enough

The Robins that sit on all the cards
The Holly the ivy, the chocolate roulade
The baubles that shine hanging from a twig
The once a year singers doing their comeback gig

Enough of the tinsel enough of the trees
Enough of the songs sung straight at me
I don't need a day to say 'you're my friend'
I just need a smile and a hug in the end

It's Christmas they chant in manic display
And everything gets more glitter each day
But please people just take time to remember
It's not Christmas yet it's bloody November

10 Blue Butterfly

I sit and gaze upon the flowers
Such beauty to behold
The tiny sweet forget-me-not
The vibrant marigold
The pansy with its happy face
Petunias bright and bold
The joyful gardens floral space
has more treasures to unfold
A beautiful blue butterfly
Flitters amongst the scene
A busy little honey bee
They really are not mean
And down under the cooling rock
The insects gather to play
A spider spins its pretty web
So it can catch its prey
And in return a sparrow sees
Which morsel it may like
It chose a fly upon the breeze
It catches with a spike
Above a hawk circles around
Sees a bunny for a meal
And down it swoops without a sound
Prey gone, just left a squeal
The beauty and the tragedy
Go hand in hand its true
But still I smile and watch the dance
Of the butterfly that's blue

Chapter Two

A Journey through Grief

Fair warning ..This chapter deals with
some difficult subjects. Please skip if you
are of a sensitive nature

Chapter 2 Contents

1....Bluebells And Blossom
2....The Voices.
3....The Numb.
4....The Black.
5....Momentum Is Key.
6....Play The Game.
7....The Scream.
8....The Fight For Fire.
9....I Don't Understand.
10...Hug Is The Drug
11...Nomed
12...That Day
13...Demons In The Shade
14...Hug The World

1 Bluebells and Blossom

Bluebells and blossom and frolicking lambs
You walk down the lane of a traveling man
When fixing your mind you do what you can
The lambs are so sweet, the flowers so pretty
They call me to write this short little ditty
But bluebells and blossom and frolicking lambs
cannot replace the loss of a man
I broke my body and he broke my mind
Relief from the tears is what I cannot find
So I turn on my heels and I bid them farewell
And go on my way in my lonely hell
I walk back to the town and I call in the pub
The music was pumping and God that felt good
So I bought me a whisky and sat myself down
and started to lose that permanent frown
Ah bluebells and blossom and frolicking lambs
when fixing your mind you do what you can
So I stayed where I was amongst strangers so kind
and I let the musicians get me out of this bind
The crooner who sings such a sad soulful song
He helps me believe nothing is wrong
The nutter who jumps and shouts "Are we drunk yet?"
He plays like a demon but I'm not done yet
The angel who sings with a voice warm and true
And still yet my Darling I'm so missing you

Ah bluebells and blossom and frolicking lambs when fixing
your mind you do what you can
So I go on my way when the show is all done
I make my way home in the bright morning sun
My purse it is empty, my tears are all gone
I'm worn out and hungry for food and for hugs but
I just walk in the door and collapse on the rug,
I dream of bluebells and blossom and frolicking lambs
I'm fixing my mind and I do what I can

2   The Voices

The voices they whisper, The voices they shout
My conscience is one of this there's no doubt
But what of the others invading my brain?
Echos of past? Or am I just insane?

Or are they the link to ancestors gone
The ones that did rise and go into the sun
Or are they the beast, my subconscious so dark
That brings my mood down when I'm in the park

Or are they the angels guiding me true
But maybe just madness cause I'm missing you
I just know each moment I'm never alone
And they are all loudest when I'm in my home

So I go where its loud just to find me some peace
I don't want to hear the call of the beast
The angels may guide but I know the way
The ancestors can talk but please not today

Just leave me alone let me sing my rock songs
Let me think for myself I'm not doing wrong
My conscience my friend let me rest let me sleep
I know that tomorrow again I will weep

I believe deep down you are all being kind
but for sanitys sake I must leave you behind
I need no chaperone, I need no advice
so sounds in my head I put you on ice
I'm back in control do you understand why?
I'm still unbroken
The Phoenix will fly

3   The Numb

Teflon skin keep hurt in
Scared of the numb don't let it win
I need to feel, I need to cry
I need the pain to wonder why
What did I do? why did he die?
Why am I punished? Oh why? oh why?
The ping of the hair as it pulls from your scalp
The sweet taste of iron as you bite in your mouth
The warm comfy feel as you beat on your thigh
What did I do? Why did he die?
The sweet slice of iron as blade cuts your skin
I'm scared of the numb I won't let it win
The grip of your nails as they gouge in your arm
Ah dammit I know they call this self harm
But no this is not this is fighting the death
That comes when alone and nothing is left
No comforting voice, no warm loving hugs
No music to soothe oh heavens above
"Get a grip bitch" I say to myself
"Stop being a child, man up, shake yourself
You are strong, you are tough, just look what you've done
You've accomplished so much you've a beautiful Son"
But still it creeps back the black cloud of numb
And I beat on my thigh like it's a drum
And I pull on my hair til I find sweet release
And sometimes I grip till my nails cut me deep
I just need hugs and a focus that's true

So I have my Cajon and I freak to a tune
I remember my past how I rocked the cello
And yeah maybe soon I revisit that fellow
So focus I must and keep a calm mind
Please help me my friends,
sing me songs, hold me close
I will get through this mess, I have to, I must
I will write it all down and try not to frown
And alcohol wise, I will try keep it down
This poem was hard to admit my bad head
But soon I do hope I'll enjoy going to bed
To the place that is honest the place that it true
Ah damn numb again
Oh babe I miss you

4 The Black

The Black creeps in like a mortal sin.
The numbing clouds, sadness begin.
All colour gone, joy left behind.
The Black chokes all within your mind.
It twists your thoughts, it's so unkind.
The dark fog hides all that heals.
It suffocates but its not real.
Its an illusion of hate and pain.
Will I ever feel like me again?
No more sun, no flowers,
I keep crying for hours.
I cannot laugh, I cannot smile.
The Black kills love all the while.
It starts as a mist, only slight but exists,
And then it builds with each sad thought.
Growing thicker and darker, poisoning my heart.
I cannot feel, I cannot love.
I cannot breathe, oh heavens above.
There is no hope, there is no cure.
The Black is too strong for me to endure.
I've no desire to eat or to sleep.
I just sit and drink and hopelessly weep.
And then in the fog a chink of light.
Just enough to help me fight.
Oh wow, a smile, and a warm hug.
A weapon to fight this blackout bug.
I see the amazing dazzling smile.
And the Black doth fade for a little while.

The warmest hug soothes the blood
I'm starting to win, I'm feeling good
Death to the Black, death to the fog
Today I will win but it's not gone for good
The black fog of gloom is a terrible beast
It is vanquished for now, for today at least
Tomorrow who knows? I'll be fine for a while
Especially if I see that dazzling smile

5   Momentum is key

Ride on the wind, ride on the rails
If you just keep on moving nothing will fail
A step to the north, a train to the south
And always yes always momentum is key
and always it will be for me

I'm scared to be still, I'm scared of the dark
I just keep on moving to protect my heart
A travellers lust, a gypsy queen's past
The old tag long gone but the blood still remains
And always yes always momentum is key
And always it will be for me

My heart knows the way my mind has no clue
But trust to my instinct is what I always do
So I'll ride on the bikes and I'll ride on the bus
I'll get off and hike as to move I just must
And always yes always momentum is key
And always it will be for me

When distance has stopped and I'm done for the day
My feet keep on moving it's the price that I pay
If I cannot travel I'll still have to move
So dance then I must and get into the groove
Because always yes always momentum is key
And always it will be for me

So smile at my dancing and laugh while I bop
If you think that I care then no not a jot
I love the moving I just can't be still
so curse me and sneer and do what you will
Because always yes always momentum is key
And always it will be for me

So at end of day and setting of sun
you will see the moon rise and night time has come
And all the earth knows the fact that is true
Always yes always momentum is key
and always it will be for me

6   Play the Game

Play the game move along
Cry again to a different song
Life is hard this is true
Feel the pain to begin anew

A loss felt deep I just can't sleep
But I move along and faith I keep
in life and love and friendships found
And other things more profound

Play the game move along
Cry again to a different song
Another day another town
I walk in the sun to stop feeling down

I see the trees I love the flowers
The birds, my friends, high in the boughs
Life is hard this is true
I feel the pain to begin anew

I take a trip through my mind
Searching for memories kind
Instead of horror, instead of woe
I am brave and there I must go

So play the game, move along,
Cry again to a different song
Remember life, remember love,
Remember laughs and stupid stuff

Hold on to that with all my might
Keep the horror back it's such a fight
but life is hard this is true
I feel the pain to begin anew

I lost the way I'm ashamed to say
But the light was seen and I'm on my way
To change the rules I have new tools
So I play the game and move along
and sing again to a different song

I knew I was ok all along

7 The Scream

Pain in my head, an inner voice that screams
I focus elsewhere instead, I need an alternative scene
I feel the demon inside. She is clawing to get out
To rip open my hide, It's coming soon there's no doubt
I cannot let that happen, I must not succumb
If anyone met that woman, I would truly be undone
How can I win this war, of me against me?
Its so hard
My focus tuned to my core, but I have the final card
I scream at the world, I smash things to ease pain
The demon can't get hold, I will be me again
I will dance and I will sing, I will laugh
I will love, I will do anything
To keep me up above
Then the bad news hits. Another light gone out
No, No, I won't quit, my resolve is stout
But still I hear the scream and feel the tearing claws
Ive little self esteem and less strength of course
The battle rages on. Most will never know
Behind the smile that's a con I feel the demon grow
One day it will break loose and tear itself free
and put good me in a noose. I will cease to be
That day is not today, I still smile and sing
All believe that I'm okay
I go now to do my thing

8 The Fight for Fire

Why does being happy cause me to be sad?
The see saw effect is really rather bad
I'm flying high, loving life
Then I'm back down a grieving wife
What can I do to level this out?
I laugh and joke then I scream and shout
I've tried being calm, a quiet mouse
But that is not me so I leave the house
The little things that trigger the pain
They wipe me out time and time again
I'm trying to cheer up and stop feeling down
But I go on a hyper and act like a clown
That false high feels so real but truthfully
I know this is no real deal
If I deny my pain, my awful grief
I lock away love and my true self
I have to work through and accept the hurt
It is so hard but it's all that will work
So today I cry, today I smile
Today I sit and wonder why this takes so long
I need it done, to get back in the sun
Out of the dark, away from the black
I can't find my way out, there is no going back
Throw me a rope, a ray of hope
Help me climb out of the mire
Help the Phoenix regain her fire

9 I Don't Understand

Sweet reminders of days gone by
I can't stop smiling no wonder why
A messy night, secrets shared
Love and hugs, my soul laid bare
I'm happier now than I've been in years
Some special people removed my fears
The music played, the beer flowed
The love, well shared by those who know
They know all of me and things I've seen
They judge me not, treat me like a queen
I don't deserve the love I get
I've a troubled mind but they hold me yet
I don't understand what they see
In a half broken wretched woman like me
But still they smile and open their arms
I find myself seduced by his roguish charm
I fight myself and then just accept
I've a right to be happy but perhaps not just yet
There is work to be done on this tortured soul
A little more sobriety is my goal
To calm down and climb off the wheel
To stop being scared to feel, to trust
And just be me without the fuss
Then maybe I could earn the love that I'm shown
These beautiful people keep me from being alone

10 Hug is the Drug

When your body lets you down
And pain makes you frown
What can you do? See a doctor or two?
Take all the pills that make you feel ill
Alternative therapy is what I need
The medicine is there in one simple deed
The hug is a drug that's a really great call
And I'll tell you what it works quicker than all
Codeine makes you sick, Morphine twice as quick
But a hug makes me smile
releasing endorphins all the while
Feeling warm, feeling safe when the pain starts to chafe
Naproxen, paracetamol and more bloody tramadol
Side effects galore then your mood hits the floor
When you take the prescription you just need more
Sack it off girl it does you no good
Forever for me the hug is the drug
It fixes my brain and even some pain
My addiction is real I can't get enough of that feeling
That I'm cared for when my mind is reeling
While I'm climbing my way out of a grief ridden mire
A hugs all I need to take me higher
So no to naproxen, no no to codiene
Cuddle me close please don't be mean
I can cope with the pain of a body that's broken
But the hope of love in any small way
Will keep me going to the end of the day
So no Ibuprofen, no no Codeine
The hug is the Drug and that's all I need

11 Nomed

May I please introduce you to Nomed
A voice that mutters doubt and bile
This guy is forever in my head
And has been now for quite a while

Whenever I dress up for the day
Whenever I catch my reflection
Nomed feels it's totally ok
To dish out a poison injection

Right now I hear him as I read
"These words are a load of old crap"
"Call yourself a poet ha! indeed!"
And my self esteem starts to collapse

Lucky enough however for me
I have some wonderful friends
Who give me strength so I'm able to see
His evil can come to an end

You see Nomed is a niggling beast
Just a demon with his name turned around
I must not give him doubts on which to feast
I must not let him gain stronger ground

I'll just smile and look to my blessings
My man, my friends and my family
I will share my words as I'm passing
And let Nomed be who he will be

12   That Day

Some days it feels like I'm walking on air
I skip, I sing, I dance without care
I see the beauty in all I purvey
But I'm sorry today is just not that day

Some days I'm pensive, thoughtful and calm
Working out my next plan with my man on my arm
I do all that I can to keep harm far away
But I'm sorry my friends today is just not that day

Some days I'm just tired like I have a cold
I creak and I groan feel like I'm getting old
All the vigor of youth seems so far away
No I'm sorry for this, this is still not that day

Today is the day the sky crushes me down
I can't do anymore but exist with a frown
I'm exhausted, I cry, fatigue whips me away
But I know deep inside it is only one day

Tomorrow is calling a beacon of hope
A light in the distance saying" stop it you dope
You are strong, you are loved, don't throw it away"
Yes hang on as tomorrow will soon be THAT day

13 Demons in the Shade

As Luna shuts her silvery eye
On a moody night like this
I think of witches flying high
And magic in the mists

I think of demons in the shade
Of trolls under the bridge
This is the time nightmares are made
As we comfort eat the fridge

The little fairies fly around
With needle fangs to bite
Then crash, a sudden sound
Oh no it's such a fright

I chase away the Grindylow
That hides beneath my bed
And realise I ought to know
It's all just in my head

14   Hug the World

At the end of the day what matters to you?
This question defines your whole life
Is it the notes in your hand or the stone in your shoe
Or the look in the eyes of a person in strife

The world at large is a very cruel place
That most of us thankfully don't understand
The knocks can floor you at relentless pace
While you smile like everythings grand

My friends I don't mean to bring you down
I just want a moment of thought
I'm sorry if my words make you frown
No I lie, now that I have you caught

Because all I ask is a moment to pause
To consider your fellow human
how would you be if you follow this course
Of never giving a damn

I'm sorry If I've been very obtuse
I have tried to find the words to say
If I'm a poet then what's the use
If I may not use it this way?

So simply put without stress
I just want our spirit to unfurl
With love, life and togetherness
Damn I wish I could just hug the world

Chapter Three

The Love of Music

Chapter 3 Contents

1....Bang On The Drum
2....Hard Rock And Roll
3....Whisky
4....Hostess
5....The Love Of Music
6....Thank You For The Music
7....Music Fest
8....Music Magic
9....When the Party's Over
10...Whisky Sweet
11...Giggle

1 Bang on the Drum

Bang on the drum, have some fun
Beast is away, I'm not undone
Slap that box, hit that tone
Keep that beat it's methadone
Stamp out the shame, beat out the rhythm
Keep it real but feelings hidden
Work out the pain work out your fears
Work your way back just to being sane
It's not reality it's all a game
Of life well lived in the fast lane
So bang the drum have some fun
Slap that box until you come undone
Feel the rhythm feel the beat
Feel the pain there's no defeat
Hit it smooth, hit it fast, hid it hard
And then at last
you'll feel the pulse of life itself
You'll feel alive like no time else
Now in the moment now as I beat
The Phoenix is rising burning her feet
On ashes of failure, on embers of pain
On cinders of regret
And an all engulfing flame
And I bang on the drum having some fun
The Phoenix doth fly
Past life is done
Forward I go
Future I come

2   Hard Rock and Roll

Sat at the bar, whisky in hand
Waiting so keen for the sound of the band
I'm hours early but I just don't care
I'll wait for the sounds I have to be there
I need the rhythm, I need the beat
I just can't stop the tapping of feet
It tugs at my heart, it pulls at my soul
That loud and crazy hard rock and roll
It's an addiction I'm just not right
Until I have danced all through the night
Until the dawn feeding the beast
That lives in my chest and gives me so much heat
I feed him in day and I feed him at night
But I am his slave and I cannot fight
The yearning I feel when life is quiet
My beast inside just wants to riot
Wants me to scream wants me to yell
wants me to beat my thighs until ...well!
This is gutteral, this is raw
This is primal and what is more
I am a slave, I have no control
and all because of hard rock and roll
Don't try to save me, don't even ask why
Just accept the phoenix must fly
High on the notes, high on the beat
High on the fire, moving her feet
If I stay here I surely will burn

With such sweet desire that I'm yet to learn
I'll just fly higher up to the sun
I'm still unbroken but maybe undone
"It's hard rock and roll girl" hell yeah I'll come
I'll come for the music, I'll come for the beat
You know I'll be there moving my feet
The Phoenix will fly her heart all aflame
Then I will collapse panting that name
I'm satisfied in sweet afterglow
Its hard rock and roll
and its all that I know

3 Whisky

Pretty glass, amber glow, warm and smooth
The friend I know
The fire stirs, it warms my heart
loosens my mind like melting snow
The scent of peat on smoky heather
My dark thoughts gone forever
And all of that in one first sip
The rest of the glass is a dangerous trip
As the fluid drains down my eager throat
My brain starts swimming like on a moat
But it's all good I feel no remorse
I will let sweet whisky take its course
It numbs my pain, the hurt, the shame
They all dissolve it's what I gain
All problems solved at least for an hour
Who knew a beverage had such power
She keeps me calm she keeps me sweet
That pretty glass just looks so neat
And then another takes its place
Down the rabbit hole I fall
Head swimming face grinning
as for friends I love them all
Ah delicious drug so sublime
for a short while the world is mine
And then she turns she screws your beliefs
That dangerous woman will not compete
You accept her forever. You take her to bed
Damn you lady whisky
you just killed my head

4 Hostess

I've not been writing, there has been no need
I'm really loving life there are no warnings to heed
I've returned to where my life began
This life of a hostess and travelling woman
The kitchen is open, the love of food expressed
The joy of providing a simple repast
It's easy it's real we all eat to heal
And it hurts if I think so I pour another drink
But to avoid all life is to avoid all hope
And I am no coward, I am no dope
I am a woman vital and true
If at all possible I will heal you
With my words, my food and maybe my touch
To make someone happy is really enough
To give me purpose, a sense of self worth
and a start on the road to erasing my hurt
So the kitchen is open, the cupboard is full
The table is groaning and tight belts undone
I'm singing and dancing and having great fun
The invite is here please friends come along

5   The Love of Music

I am so grateful I have to say
To all the weirdos and reprobates
To all free thinkers and music makers
You will all be acknowledged at the pearly gates

Every day I'm low is soothed by a chord or line
When this crying soul takes the persona of clown
When deep inside hell I'm crying all the time
I grab every word to reverse that frown

Every payday I look to see what can I afford?
To watch true talent and melt into the void
Most weeks the answer is no but I'm bored
I am watching the expenditure to try and avoid

But life is more than pounds and pence
It's more than next week's bill
I'm going out for my soul it makes sense
To resist will surely make me ill

6 Thank you for the Music

As a young girl all I needed was to sing
I joined a choir being noisy was my thing
My grandma taught me to feel the sound
And kept my feet firm on the ground

As a young woman I found soft rock
I found leather and lace and ditched the pop
The music started to infect my soul
And from here to feel was my only goal

You see for me music is not just sound
It's never just noise hanging around
For me it's always a physical thing
I will laugh or cry and usually sing

I can't help myself it's like a spell
Losing yourself when the vocals go well
When the guitar plays and I move my feet
And bang I'm up dancing out of my seat

I'll go to kareoke and sing a few tunes
Releasing my tension like writing runes
The voice comes out like it's not really me
And I end on a high giggling and free

Also my friends playing the old John O Gaunt
Thank you for the music in the place that I haunt
I treasure those moments of moving song
Making me feel like this odd girl belongs

I belong to the guitar, I belong to the drum
I belong to the vocals from scream to hum
I belong to the dance
The music in me leaves me in a trance
I am music
I am free

7   Music Fest

Ticker tape upon the floor
Broken glasses, so much more,
People living their best life
Causing bar staff so much strife

Yes the band is bloody ace
Yes your jumping keeps up pace
But the poor glass collector girl
Is struggling in a bloody whirl

She has to battle through the crowd
To do her job though the music's loud
To keep the bar staff able to serve
To some of these folks getting on nerves

Yes it's a wonderful time of year
So many sounds so many cheers
But spare a thought for the knackered staff
For them the week can be bloody naff

There is a chance, a little time
Before I finish off my rhyme
This is a magical music Fest
Please all behave your bloody best

8 Music Magic

A sudden song, it won't be long before the feelings start
To penetrate your guarded mind and reignite your heart
A certain type of melody, a beat, a clever line
And all at once your very world has travelled back in time
You see this is the magic, the voodoo and the hex
That every music maker has the power to possess
They can play it sweet and soulful
and make fair maidens swoon
They can weave a velvet blanket,
leave you in a warm cocoon
They can raise the mighty warrior
with the drumbeat and the fire
All the energy of their vocals lifting spirits ever higher
It has been this way forever since mankind first struck a rock
Why we feel sound deep within our core it really is no shock
There is rhythm in the music, in the dancing, in the street
There's rhythm in the body of the lovers heartbeats
There is rhythm in the waves as they crash upon the shore
Yes there is rhythm in this life and will be forever more
So pay homage to the music man pay homage to the band
What ever it is you need to feel
They have it in their hand

9 When the Party's Over

When the party's over
And the hangovers begun
we reminisce 'bout being pissed
And having so much fun

And then we grab our uniforms
And make our way to work
But the boss saw Instagram
He calls you a bloody jerk

But still we do our job of work
And finish said long day
We sulk that party time is done
Shame we now have to pay

The moral of the tale is this
When having fun with drink
The shift is long and hard
The party lasts a blink

10   Whisky Sweet

Whisky sweet whisky dry
Pain doth leave I wonder why
Whisky smokey whisky peat
Take away the arthritic heat

All the codeine in all the world
Can't compete with my whisky girl
All the "brufen" and all the "paras"
Won't ever match your after hours

So thank you lady, thank you friend
No work tomorrow I can sleep again
I know my weakness is evident
Tonight I sleep its heaven sent

11 Giggle

Tee hee hee ha ha ha
I giggle along as I go to the bar
I can't lose this smile, I can't quench the laugh
I'm joyful inside and that is a fact
I've lost my mind, my marbles are gone
I giggle away to the setting of sun
As I know the truth, a fact that was hidden
Life is a joke and I'm not even kidding
The band's make me dance and freak to the beat
If I don't get up I'll just rock out in my seat
Euphoria mine, I'm high on good times
Don't try to bring me down it just can't be done
I'm giggling away to the setting of sun
My friends give me hugs and think that I've cracked
But I'll tell you what, No! It's just that
The pain that was there, the grief, the gloom
The angry drink beast, the impending doom
They all disappeared, it's really quite wierd
I feel alive, it's more man I thrive in this place
Just look at my face see the giggling clown
Who's no longer down
I'm so grateful my friends, my tolerant mates
There have been times I've been hard to take
I'm so lucky it's true, hell all I love you
My heart fit to burst, I'm no longer cursed
The day has been won
And I'll giggle away to the setting of sun

Chapter Four

The Life of a Carer

Chapter 4 Contents

1....The Battle Of Life
2....The Carer
3.... Dementia
4....The Circle Of Pain
5....Me, Myself And I
6....Adapt
7....The Label
8.... Fatigue Trance
9.... Poo
10...Baker, Builder, Poet
11...The Bug

1 The Battle of Life

To feel real joy you must first feel pain
You can't have pretty rainbows without a little rain
You never know how high you've flown
Until you crash back down to earth
You don't need illegal drugs my friend
to understand that hurt
But sometimes pain builds up
And gets you deep inside
Then on that downward spiral once again I slide
So out of town I run and on a bus I ride
To join a stormy lake and on its waves I glide
The wind it whips my hair, the rain it stings my face
And slowly smiles return and I start to win the race
For its a marathon of grief, its no short little sprint
I've many miles to run but today I slow my feet
I've many tricks that I employ to keep the beast below
From wrecking all that I enjoy, it does come close I know
My head gets in such turmoil, the little things build up
I get so bloody paranoid then too much ale I sup
I know these are my weaknesses. Please believe that I do try
To fight the angry beast inside that makes me cry and cry
But back to positivity, to thoughts that calm my brain
Some really seem to care, so I fight that beast again
I'll battle hard and battle well with all weapons I possess
The music, dance and hugs from friends
are among the very best
Sometimes I lose my way as every journeyman does
I'll find my path again someday
and regain my happy buzz

2 The Carer

The work is hard, the work is long
And nothings as it seems
1 change their beds I clean their clothes
And keep their faces clean
The days roll by one after another
I watch them cry time and again
For life gone by, a long lost lover
So then I'm moved to get my pen
For I'm in pain my back it hurts
The alarm bell rings again
This cycle is the carers curse
to walk in dark and rain
To live my life to serve the needs of our elderfolk
And keep my cheerful verve it really is a joke
I don't know how not to care
I don't even want to try
I just know I have to be there until the day they die
I'm weary and I'm worn out, my social life is nil
I've nothing in my bank account
ouch ill take another pill
So off again I go to take their daily chores
Old woman and old men
if you need me I'm yours

3   Dementia

Today I'm 14 and I work the cotton mill
In the card room I'm placed and work with my twin
The boss is great and I love my task
The big bell rings and now I'm back
Now I'm 91 and I cant feel my feet
I giggle with nurses they think I'm sweet
So I eat my meal and I drink my drink
Lunchtime is over and now I need to sleep
When I wake I know I'm late
I ought to be at the factory gate
Its hard when you're 30 and have a family to support
My man is at war, we all do what we hate
So I stand to get ready and what?
What is this? My feet wont work
Oh how I'm tired of this
Ouch the pain "sit down" they say
The factory was then its not open today
For a moment I know truth
I'm 91 and I've lost my youth
But my head plays games and I travel back in time
The nurses they tell me everything's fine
So I cry for lost times and I wish I was gone
My life has been long
I want to reach for the sun
I call for my twin I call for my mum
I have dementia
Its really no fun

4 The Circle of Pain

The circle of pain is the crux of life
From birth to the grave its the same
Every day is more trouble and strife
Every year we begin it again
We start our journey in a screaming fit
We emerge bloody and angry it's true
The midwives try to do their bit
To stop us returning blue
A while later we try to walk
It hurts as we build muscles new
But still we persist and grow on in our lives
Its all that we know how to do
And then we arrive all gangly and grown
Our tendons screaming in pain
All the teenage angst we need to purge
But we suffer on still again
And then comes the keenest hurt of all
The agony of love declined
To pick yourself up just to fall
That's the real pain that makes you cry
So into our dotage we finally come
All aches and hurt again
The reaper opens the pearly gates
And all this life seems in vain

You suffer and moan all your days long
You really didn't have a clue
all you need is a smile and a song
Just have love in your heart keep it true

Because pain is really your friend
The hurt tells no lies
you feel alive and you'll find in the end
It's the numb you truly despise

without pain you cannot feel love
Without love you may as well be dead
Just remember this absolute truth
Pain is all in your head

5 Me, Myself and I

With nothing to do in a room with no view
It's time to ponder what lies within
It's a difficult task, very hard to do
I don't even know how to begin
I guess for a start I'll look in my heart
I am the warrior you see
I am brave and strong and stand apart
But that's not all I can be
For myself is wise knows the turn of the sky's
The rhythm of the moon and the trees
Myself likes to learn, she really tries
She thinks knowledge sets her free
But there in the corner quiet and scared
Is the young child that is me
She is creative, all innocence bared
The most vulnerable of all of the three
"Let's go" said I, not caring why
When myself understood the design
As little me just needs love you see
So all three can truly feel fine
The moral is this, said all three with a hiss
We work together or not at all
So all facets unite in hopefull bliss
Its me myself and I and that's all

6 Adapt

The only thing constant in life is change
From birth to death we adapt
If something is wrong simply rearrange
Like someone said put on a new hat
The world doesn't halt so why do we
Get so comfy in our safe rut
Look around my friends and you will see
You probably need a kick up the butt
When your reality becomes like an ocean
And your drifting on your safe boat
Pretty soon they'll be storms up ahead
And you need to learn how to keep afloat
Im sorry my friend if I have mislead
I have no real answer you see
This is just some junk come out of my head
Think Im kinda insane you see
But I've been alive half a century now
And I'm convinced I should share a few thoughts
To all that indulge me I take a bow
And thank every small battle I fought
As every fight teaches a skill
however subtle and small
Every single soul can adapt at will
I have total faith in you all

7 The Label

And off she goes in her worn out clothes
Wondering what the day will bring
Will it be hard on her and her bones
Or will she smile and sing?
Her world is a void as she starts the day
Her routines provide the structure
The chaos of strife is not ok
She is tempted to read some scripture
But onward she goes nevertheless
To the workplace to lend her heart
To the tired, the desperate and under duress
She has been carer right from the start
The role she has chosen is this
Give your time your compassion and love
Take the abuse without even a hiss
Hoping someone smiles from above
And the end of shift she limps home
Then her personal life can begin
All those worries and fears that she owns
So much turmoil she keeps locked within
She is a pressure cooker waiting to blow
She is a bomb ticking its time
One day soon she will crack you know
Because that label of carer is mine

8 Fatigue Trance

The bedside alarm forgot to chime
And my body clock is a jerk
I woke at bloody 4am
When it's 5 I need for work
Last night was a stolen pleasure
Of music laughs then love
Magic medicine beyond measure
Then reality crashes from above
But I wouldn't change this for the world
My mini moments of mayhem
My sanity would simply fold
If I could not do this again
So off I go for another shift
Of hard work for my body and mind
I need these little mental lifts
To myself I must be kind
In conclusion folks I have to say
I need my work play balance
It's worth much more than weekly pay
It's worth the fatigue trance

9 Poo

It's been a day or maybe two
Since my backside has tried to poo
Now that's not strange or even wierd
But the mention of this act is feared
Now every person has to go
From London town to Tokyo
The variety of shit is huge
From a tiny pebble to a big brown luge
The type of crap depends on the day
What did you eat to help it's way?
Is it a pizza dough to crack that ring
Or a Guinness shit yep that's a thing
Whilst on this topic not being a fool
I learned that Bristol had a chart of poo
A perfect four is where to aim
But many craps can't say the same
The colours vary, the stench does too
The myriad of human poo
The diarrhea, the painful rain
The stomach cramps, the aweful pain
The shy ochre turtle that shows its head
but no bog nearby oh the dread
The point I think I'm trying to say
Toilet aside it's been a shit of a day

10 Builder, Baker, Poet

A builder builds his walls
A baker bakes his bread
Im a simple wordsmith
So I just write instead

The builder places all his bricks
In a way tall and strong
His craft is needed world around
To shelter us from storms

The baker such a humble guy
bakes bread to feed our needs
Without this guy we would starve
Everyone hug a baker please

And me the humble wordsmith
Have a simple job it's true
I speak the truth upon this land
What you take is up to you

I will talk about the good times
I will talk about the bad
I will gush about the silly days
And the joy and laughs we had

11   The Bug

Head is pounding, vision is blurred
Snot flows freely and time is absurd
One moment I'm cold the next I burn
All the remedies at my hand and I still need to learn
How to walk down the street looking normal at least
Hide behind the paper mask
It's a troublesome task
I'm testing and testing It comes up with a neg
Happy Easter they say
So where is my egg?
It's ok it's girl flu Or man flu what ever
I still feel poorly But it's lovely weather
Pre C word it's fine It's a cold just drink wine
But now what the hell I coughed
Ring the plague bell
Ok rant is done
Hope I'm better with rising sun
Hope you guys miss this dose
When safe I'll hold you close

Chapter Five

Pure Whimsy

Chapter 5 Contents

1....Gremlins
2....Sisters We Know
3....Brigid
4....The Wedding
5....Perfect Moments
6....Merry Christmas
7....New Year
8....Samhain
9....Halloween Queen
10...The Soul
11...Solstice
12...Candyfloss Sky
13...Pride
14...The Sad Ones
15...My Beautiful Man

1 Gremlins

I have house gremlins I do declare
When stuff goes missing I know they're there
When the thing I place on the mantle above
goes poof, then missing, oh heavens above
It doesn't matter they have their fun
If it's something you need then off they run
Your phone, your keys, your bloody specs
I hear them laughing as you're vexed
Damn you gremlins you mean no harm
But that fall nearly broke my bloody arm
Why is a conker on my stairs
Turning me into a Northern Pam Ayres?
My Grandma said to ask St Anthony
if ever stuff was lost to me,
but Grandma no these guys arn't him
and I suspect they hate a hymn
Truth be told they love mischief
I love them dearly, I have no beef
Just if I ask when joke is done
Let me find the thing that is gone
My naughty little gremlins of house
Keep me on my toes as well as my spouse
Keep us knowing that you are here
And we will keep a careful ear
The fae that are about and abound
Are never truly underground
So I light a candle late at night
And ask please reveal things lost from sight

2 Sisters we know

Sisters we know the rule of three
What 'ere we give out returns to thee
The veil is thin, the moon is full
I have had enough of this damn bull
Protect your loved ones. Protect the earth.
Give all your might for what it's worth
I speak through love, I protect from pain
We need the community back again
Pray with me, please raise your glass
Let's kick this oppression in the ass
Come together on this book of face
Let's reinvent the human race
No time to fear this c word plague
When all the answers are dull and vague
So stand up proud reclaim your life
Yeah the bug is bad but damn my life
When did we lose our sense of worth
When did we shun our friends
The weakest folk that walked the earth
Victimised!
Where will it end?

3 Brigid

Brigid toss your ginger hair
A little snow here, a little frost there
But just below the frigid crust
The plants break ground just as they must.

The tantalising glimpse of life
That helps us face our troubles and strife
The moon so full with cheerful gleam
Life's never so bleak as it seems

So welcome friends, turn away woe
We will gain strength, watch as we grow
We will be strong as the tall trees
We only rest, not brought to knees

We rise again in the morning sun
The spring is coming, new life begun
Welcome Brigid, welcome friend
Together we see this winters end

4　The Wedding

And finally it came to pass
The witch hooked the ginger
And she married that ass
The bride wore black, the groom nearly swooned
And all was done in a nearly empty room

The attendants to be fair were not your usual clan
We had a fella in heels and a wicca green man
And then family members not understanding why
we have a punk dressed like a lady
and a witch joined on the fly

But the day went well and we all had a laugh
And much beer flowed in this amazing gaff
Nick and Leanne are joined in law
And all had fun like so many times before

The music played, it was loud and happy
The bride even danced with her drunken pappy
The crowds all cheered with reckless abandon
And many maids outfits had a malfunction

All in all twas an epic day
All seemed happy no tears today
And true to form as a parting treat
The bride left her knee skin on the street

5   Perfect Moments

Perfect moments are
Like when the moon hits the sea
Like when the leaves whisper your name
Like when it's just you and me

Perfect moments are
Like when the sun warms your face
Like when the whisky soothes your throat
Like when I'm lost in your embrace

Perfect moments are
When the stars guide your way
When the stream giggles along
When we kiss at end of day

Perfect moments are
Just this, our brief time
A glimpse of true joy
And a whimsical rhyme

Perfect moments are
Sadly too soon gone
Open your wanting heart
Here comes another one

6   Merry Christmas

Sitting here with another sore head
Caused by bad music and a cold
I wonder why coke turned our santa red
What was wrong with the green man of old?

When did the pesky elf become a thing?
With his many stupid pranks
I just want a sleigh bell to ring
And folks that remember to say thanks

A simple small token as gift is great
Given with love after a meal
Not an expensive gadget you soon learn to hate
That was bought because of a 'great deal'

The cash that's spent on things not required
Is usually vanity led
It's time to get our brains rewired
And learn some gratitude instead

All I want this year by miles
my favorite gifts, only three
Is the health the happiness and smiles
Of my Love, my friends and my family

Merry Christmas

7 New Year

The years keep turning round and around
Another notch on the wheel of life
So many folks yearning for a loving sound
Here is what I need, more peace, less strife

Its just one day, one notch on the calendar
Though we place such import on our dates
We think it will impact so much, so far
Its a start we think to improve our fates

But truth be told its all just junk
Same old stuff same old way
Maybe use the words of punks of old
Sid vicious said he did it 'my way'

Its been hard my friends I know it's true
This C word fight. yet again its tough
But hell you know, we will see it through
I Love you guys, when is enough, enough?

"Enough" I say to cold and alone
"Enough" I say to leaning to vice
My friends please remember to use the phone
Let's put all this heartache and pain on ice

8 Samhain

Witches and ghosts and little black cats
Sweeties and pumpkins and loads of naff tatt
Scary old films watched late after dark
And a wonderful chill
As you walk through the park
This is the time when all is aglow
From sunset at tea to the cheeks on your beau
This is the time when I feel alive
Halloween again I could jump, I could jive
These are the days to party with friends
Parkin and toffee the fun never ends
Mulled wine and cider, the beer on a tap
But please keep away that damn santa hat
We can costume its a thing don't you know
We can gather around and make a great show
This is not Christmas
No this is not that again I say
No to the damn santa hat
Be gentle good friends you may see a spook
Or maybe just curl up with a good book
I'll say it once and I'll say it again
Blessed be my friends
This is Samhain

9 Halloween Queen

It's Halloween the Queen is here to shake vanilla souls
To pumpkin spice the bourbon ice
Let's revisit our life goals
Age 10, I thought I knew it all
Dadda tought me the game of chess
I learned to think my way out of situations of duress
Age 18 I became the queen of leather, lace and love
But grandma kept my soul in check"the answers are above"
Age 30, now I'm momma
All the trials that gives and takes
My one true achievement in life my boy I'm so proud it aches
Age 40, well don't wanna say too much
Tough times those who know know
But even in the times of hurt our souls learn how to grow
Age 46, life implodes
How did this happen to me I should have known
I am the witch It's in my family tree. The pain, the grief,
The sweet relief the feelings do a loop
And all I do is drink and cry and hope I don't get removed
Age well you know I don't wanna say
But fate has turned her face
A beautiful understanding soul
Thinks my jeans are kinda ace
So now I have a second chance
To love, to be serene
Damn right ill grasp it with both hands
I am the Halloween Queen

10 The Soul

The soul doesn't care what the body needs
What the physical form should dictate
The inside has a higher purpose indeed
Never shunning, never being irate
The soul is a powerful raging force
When engaged to fulfil its next task
It's strong and willful and on course
It forgets simply just to ask
They talk of soulmates and peaceful zen
They just don't understand this
That the soul is beyond the now and then
It's above the "that" and the" this"
This is a crazy untamed beast
That folk try to say is all nice
Nah mate give it food and it will feast
Do it wrong and you pay the price
I think what I am trying to say is this
What's inside is your absolute truth
I myself do whisper in a hushed hiss
I'm in love and I regained some youth
So friends please listen to your soul
Please feed it with love and great sounds
Make peace and love your only goal
And watch as good times abound

11 Solstice

Solstice is here with all its charms
The time is now to take your chance
Sun god open your loving arms
Lady luna dance your tranquil dance
The sun is burning on the longest day
The fire of hope and fruitfulness
The light to guide us on our way
Through every little happenstance
Lady luna opens her eyes
Graceful silver girl of night
Claiming velvet sparkling skies
Giving a welcome calming sight
And down below we mortal souls
Scurry around like ants on mud
We show no care for celestial goals
Would not slow even if we could
We rush around forever blind
To the majesty and beauty around
All the sights and smells on this earth
True joy waiting to be found
So take a breath my dear
And listen to this amazing planet
Stop a while please have no fear
We're alive be grateful god damn it

12   Candyfloss Sky

Candyfloss sky leaves me wondering why
The world looks so pretty
When so many cry
The cruelty of man
Leaves a stain on our souls
But the sweet little snowdrop
Just to bloom is its goal
I feel like I need to world to be black
At least till the monsters quit their attack
At least til a person can love the next one
Then maybe I'll accept the burgeoning sun
My heart feels so heavy,
my eyes want to weep
The human race dwindles
People dying in their sleep
But flowers brightly bloom
And trees still grow high
Love and hope chases gloom
Under that candyfloss sky

13   Pride

It matters not the skin you're in
It matters not if you're shy
Your gender your colour, be you stout or thin
Are no barrier to how you fly

The world is full of bile and hate
It's a struggle to see the joy
Who dares wins at the loving stakes
Regardless of girl or boy

True love is a pure emotion
It's the closest to heaven we get
Why suffer the drama and commotion
Mostly bourne from jealousy I bet

My thought quite simply put is this
The fact we find love inside
Against all odds and prejudice
Is the biggest reason to have pride

14 The Sad Ones

The wind is howling, the storm is here
The town is preparing for Christmas cheer
The trees going up, the baubles that glisten
The music is playing, we all go to listen
Sat in a corner the person who's sad
Thinking it's Christmas, it's really not bad
It's only a day that lasts half a year
I cannot cope, hand me a beer
The brighter the lights, the darker the shadow
The demons to fight with hotchoc and mallow
The future is rosy when bright is the sun
But darkness can soon drain away all the fun
For some this time is a history attack
When cruel memories reign and you can't get back
Lost friends, lost loves, fights round the tree
Remember my friends kind words are for free
I don't mean to whine I don't mean to bleat
I worry for those who can't afford heat
I worry for friends sat lost and alone
My plea to all is remember to phone
So stuff all the presents the fake bloody smiles
For a genuine hug I'd travel for miles
for some it's not safe, this time its not kind
When decking your tree
Bear the sad ones some mind

15 My Beautiful Man

A dazzling smile and sardonic wit
At last I'm alive, at last this is it
The years of pain melting away
My soul is soothed day after day
A beautiful man stands right by my side
He scolds me not and bolsters my pride
He looks after my brain and after my heart
I knew I'd found love right from the start
This isn't the same as a giddy teen fling
I'm a mature lady now, grey's and everything
I've too many curves and too little cash
But he doesn't mind not one slight dash
He only cares that I'm safe and I'm sound
My beautiful man has his feet on the ground
We share a sofa for hours and hours
And every so often he will bring me flowers
We love each other through and through
My world started healing when he said "I do"
My pain and my suffering are still part of me
But at last I announce
The Phoenix is free

Index

A Million Kisses 11
Adapt......,.....................................60
Autumn..7
Bang On The Drum........................39
Blue Butterfly................................14
Bluebells And Blossom...................17
Brigid..70
Builder Baker Poet..........................64
Candyfloss Sky..............................79
Dementia.......................................56
Demons In The Shade.....................35
English Sun.....................................9
Fatigue Trance...............................62
Giggle...51
Gremlins..68
Halloween Queen...........................76
Hard Rock And Roll.......................40
Hostess..43
Hug Is The Drug............................32
Hug The World..............................36
I Asked The North Wind..................8
I Don't Understand.........................31
I Wish I Had A Garden.....................4
Love Is In The Detail......................10
Me Myself And I............................59
Merry Christmas............................73
Momentum Is Key..........................25
Music Fest.....................................47
Music Magic.................................48
My Beautiful Man.....…................…..82
New Year......................................74

83

Index continued

Nomed..33
Perfect Moments................................72
Play The Game....................................27
Poo...63
Pride..80
Samhain..75
Sisters we know..................................69
Solstice...78
Sprinkles..13
Sunshine..12
Thank You For The Music..................45
That Day...34
The Battle of life.................................54
The Black...23
The Bug..65
The Carer...55
The Circle Of Pain..............................57
The Fight For Fire..............................30
The Label...61
The Love Of Music.............................44
The Numb..21
The Sad Ones.....................................81
The Scream...29
The Soul...77
The Storm..6
The Voices 19
The Wedding.......................................71
When The Party's Over......................49
Whisky..42
Whisky Sweet......................................50

84

Printed in Great Britain
by Amazon